MOM MOM MAKES A U-TURN

WRITTEN BY DALE G. ORMAN ED.D
ILLUSTRATIONS BY CHARLES W. HICKMAN

to Jordan, David and Sander-
Mommom loves you!

It all began one spring day. Mommom and I were going away.

We started out at map point A...
Then went to B...so far, Okay!

We passed a park,
stopped at the zoo...
Just as we're supposed to do.

At point C Mommom
made a right...
And ended at a red stop light.

We found points E and F and G...
Imagine what we got to see.

We passed a beach and ocean too.
We turned left, again we knew...

We viewed some houses
and some trees.
We saw birds, flies,
gnats and bees.

We see points K, L, M, and N.
Oh my gosh, we're lost again.

**There's map points O,P,Q and R
Again we don't know
where we are.**

So we make u-turn number 4...
Please Mommom don't
do anymore.
Driving by S, T and U...
This mountain makes a
lovely view.

We pass a barn, flowers and grass...
U-turn 5, we're low on gas!

Passing shops V, W, X and Y...
Don't stop Mommom...
Please let's drive by.

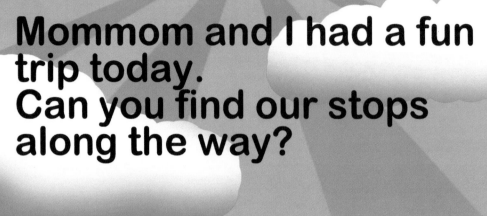

Mommom and I had a fun trip today.
Can you find our stops along the way?

MOM MOM MAKES A U-TURN